Sukaq and the Raven

by Roy Goose and Kerry McCluskey

Artwork by Soyeon Kim

For River

Published by Inhabit Media Inc. · www.inhabitmedia.com
Inhabit Media Inc. (Iqaluit), P.O. Box 11125, Iqaluit, Nunavut, X0A 1H0
(Toronto), 191 Eglinton Avenue East, Suite 301, Toronto, Ontario, M4P 1K1

Design and layout copyright © 2017 Inhabit Media Inc.
Text copyright © 2017 Roy Goose and Kerry McCluskey
Artwork copyright © 2017 Soyeon Kim
Photography by Jay Enzi © 2017 Inhabit Media Inc.

Editors: Neil Christopher and Kelly Ward
Art director: Danny Christopher

We acknowledge the support of the Canada Council for the Arts for our publishing program.

This project was made possible in part by the Government of Canada.

Printed in Canada.

Library and Archives Canada Cataloguing in Publication

McCluskey, Kerry, 1968-, author
    Sukaq and the raven / by Kerry McCluskey and Roy Goose
; artwork by Soyeon Kim.

ISBN 978-1-77227-139-3 (hardcover)

I. Goose, Roy, author II. Kim, Soyeon, illustrator III. Title.

PS8625.C62S85 2017   jC813'.6   C2017-904226-2

Sukaq and the Raven

by Roy Goose and Kerry McCluskey

artwork by Sayeon Kim

In a tiny community called Apex in Nunavut, there was a boy named Sukaq who was sweet and fast and who had an imagination that led him on all sorts of adventures.

Sukaq loved listening to stories before bed, because sometimes the stories followed him into his dreams. He would curl up beside his *anaana* and listen to her as he drifted off to sleep.

4

His favourite story was about the raven creating the world. It always gave him the best dreams because he imagined he was flying high in the sky on the raven's wings.

5

Anaana began, "This is a bedtime story that I heard from a friend of mine, who heard it from his grandmother, who also heard it from someone else. This story is very, very old. One day, there was a raven flying all by himself. This was an absolutely enormous raven: the biggest raven that ever, ever existed."

This is the part of the story that excited Sukaq the most. As he listened to his anaana, he closed his eyes and imagined himself sitting on the giant raven's back, right between his wings, holding on tightly, climbing higher and higher. As the raven and Sukaq flew into the dark night sky, it started to snow.

The raven spread his wings and said, "I'd sure like to rest. I've been flying forever."

The absolutely enormous raven started to glide. As he glided, snow gathered on his wings and he tipped over to one side. Sukaq could feel himself tipping to one side with the raven, and he dug his hands even deeper into the raven's feathers. He caught cold snowflakes on his tongue and laughed as the raven glided through the sky. What a ride!

The snow started to fall from the raven's higher wing to his lower wing, and a little avalanche began. A ball of snow gathered and rolled right toward Sukaq. He ducked just in time, and when the giant snowball reached the end of the other wing, the raven flung it out into space.

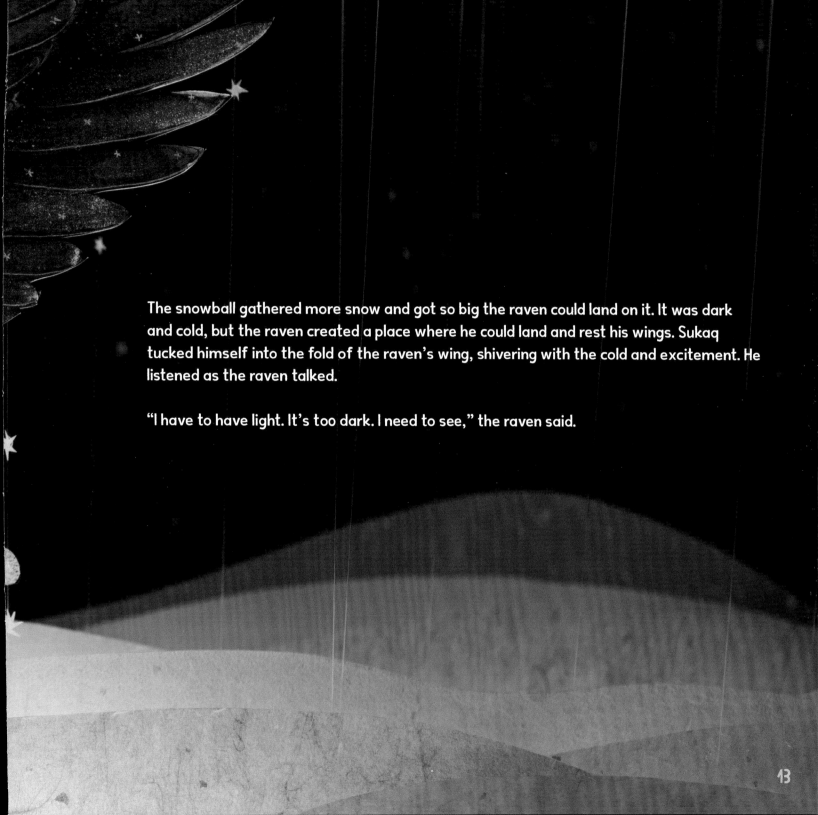

The snowball gathered more snow and got so big the raven could land on it. It was dark and cold, but the raven created a place where he could land and rest his wings. Sukaq tucked himself into the fold of the raven's wing, shivering with the cold and excitement. He listened as the raven talked.

"I have to have light. It's too dark. I need to see," the raven said.

So the raven pecked at the ground and a plant started growing. The raven could see something very bright growing inside the plant. The raven grabbed the bright object and flung it into the sky. That became the sun. Sukaq squinted against the glare, but he was glad for the warmth and the light.

Later, as the sun set, the raven said the night was too dark and he needed light to see. Sukaq was glad because even though he was a very brave boy, he was still a little bit afraid of the dark. The raven pecked at the ground and another plant came out of the earth. There was a silvery light inside the plant. The raven grabbed the shiny object and flung it into the sky. That became the moon. Sukaq loved the moon, especially when it was big and full, as it was now.

The raven found his roost for the evening and soon went to sleep with Sukaq tucked safely under his wing. As Sukaq drifted off, his makeshift bed of raven feathers felt just as comfortable as his cozy bed at home.

When Sukaq and the raven awoke, the raven said, "I need a partner on earth."

He pecked at the ground and a third plant grew. He pecked at the plant and, when it opened up, there was a human inside. The raven breathed life into the human's nostrils, and it became a woman.

The raven told the woman, "I am your partner."

The woman said, "No, you are not. You are a raven."

The raven replied, "Watch me." He stood straight up and his raven form folded back and a man appeared. His wings turned into a beautiful parka.

Sukaq's fingers let go of the man's parka and he fell to the ground with a thump so strong that it shook him awake out of his dream. He opened his eyes and looked at his anaana. He wasn't flying around, creating the world with a giant raven. He was tucked into bed.

"And that's how the raven created the universe," Anaana said. "Now, sleep well, Sukaq. Tomorrow is another day with another adventure."

And the boy who was sweet and fast and loved to dream fell back asleep.

Afterword

Thanks to Inuvialuit oral culture and the many hours of stories Mamayauk passed on to us to preserve for future generations. And to Kerry McCluskey for her due diligence and great storytelling.

—Roy Goose

This is a story I heard from Roy Goose in 1999. I travelled to Inuvik, Northwest Territories, to record stories about ravens, and Roy was on my list of people to visit. I'd already known Roy for a few years and knew him to be an engaging and charismatic storyteller. He had many tales to tell, some of which appear in *Tulugaq*, a book published by Inhabit Media in 2013. Roy's creation story is pure magic and forms the basis of this story, *Sukaq and the Raven*. Roy told me he learned the creation story and many more from his great-grandmother, Mamie Mamayauk.

—Kerry McCluskey

Roy Goose learned many of the legends he knows from his great-grandmother, Mamie Mamayauk, who was born in 1885 in Kittigakyuit at the mouth of the Mackenzie River and travelled with the Arctic explorer Vilhjalmur Steffansson. Roy passed his legends on to his children to teach them important life lessons and morals.

Kerry McCluskey lived in Yellowknife, Northwest Territories, for five years before moving to Iqaluit, Nunavut, in 1998 to work as a journalist. Nearly twenty years later, Kerry continues to write and has built a wonderful home in Iqaluit with her son, River Talittuq Sukaq Gordon McCluskey. Her son features prominently in many of the stories she tells.

Soyeon Kim is a Toronto-based, Korean-born artist and art educator who specializes in work that merges fine sketching and painting techniques to produce three-dimensional dioramas. Her previous children's books include *Wild Ideas*, *Is This Panama?*, and *You Are Stardust*, for which she won the Amelia Frances Howard-Gibbon Illustrator's Award.

Iqaluit • Toronto